Cortez the Gnome

by Amadee Ricketts and James Orndorf

Published by Canyon Largo Press
Durango, CO 81301
www.cortezthegnome.com
amadee@cortezthegnome.com

Hand lettering and map illustration by Clint Reid.
See more of Clint's work at www.tillmanproject.com

ISBN 978-0-692-41422-4

For Allegra, Luck, and all the kids who helped Cortez along the way.

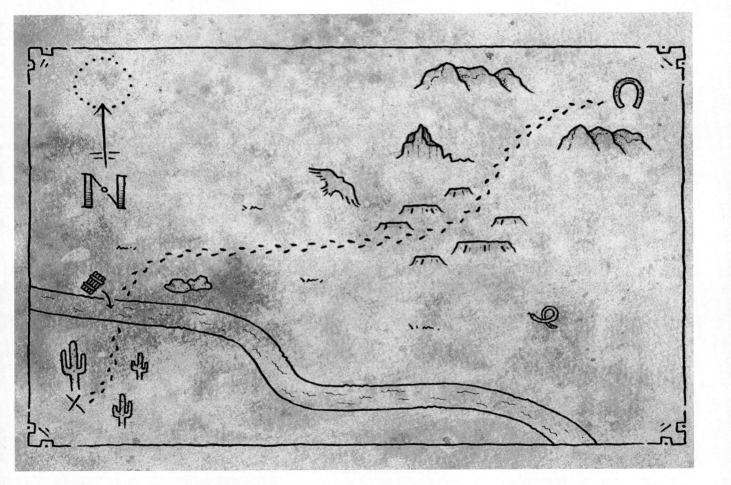

One day, not too long ago, Cortez the gnome headed for home.

When he arrived at his big shaggy juniper tree, he checked his mail box. He was hoping for a letter from his younger brother Winslow, who had left home some time ago to have an adventure.

Cortez missed Winslow terribly. So every day he checked his mail box, only to find it empty. But today was different. Today, there was a letter. A letter from Winslow!

Dear Cortez,

How are you? I have missed you very much. I have finally found a new home, and I have so many things to tell you. Please come visit me as soon as you can. It is a long way, so I have drawn a map.

Your brother,
Winslow

Cortez loved his tree and his cozy bed. He loved knowing that every day would be pretty much the same. But he loved his brother Winslow most of all. He would set out for Winslow's house the next day.

That night he was so excited that he could hardly get to sleep. When he finally drifted off, he dreamt of adventures, and of Winslow.

First thing the next morning, he started getting ready for his trip. He wrote to Winslow, and began to pack all the things a gnome might need to have a real adventure.

But a gnome can only carry so much.

Cortez filled his backpack with the few things he needed most. He tied on a bedroll, a cooking pot, and an extra pair of boots. Last of all, he added Mr. Frog, Winslow's favorite toy from when he was a baby gnome. Mr. Frog would be a surprise for Winslow.

He posted a sign on his door, so that none of his animal friends would worry. Then he began walking south, over hills and across the wide, dry plains.

Traveling was dangerous for someone so small. He watched carefully for animals that might want to eat him.

Late in the day, he set up camp. He fell asleep listening to the breeze, and thinking of all the wonderful times he and Winslow had when they were young.

Cortez walked on for days, and found himself farther from home than he had ever been. He followed Winslow's map into the desert.

When he came to a towering rock that looked like a sailing ship, he recognized it from the map. He was exactly where he should be. He just needed to keep walking.

And walking. And walking some more.

And then walking just a little bit more.

After all that walking, Cortez had nearly reached the end of the map! The last thing between him and Winslow's house was a wide, muddy river.

He set right to work building a raft to get across.

On the other side of the river, Cortez began searching for the big cactus that was Winslow's house. And suddenly, he spotted Winslow!

The brothers hugged for a long time.

Winslow said, "Cortez, I have missed you so much. I am sorry it has been such a long time. There are a couple of gnomes who can't wait to meet you."

"Gnomes? But Winslow, I thought we were the only gnomes."

"I thought so too, but I was wrong. Come inside and meet my wife Daisy, and our little boy, Bloomfield!"

Cortez was an uncle! This was the happiest day he could remember.

The family talked, and sang gnome songs, and ate together. After dinner, Cortez played with baby Bloomfield until it was time for him to go to bed.

Cortez and Winslow stayed up long into the night. Winslow told the story of how he found other gnomes at last, and how he met Daisy. The brothers made plans for Winslow and his family to visit Cortez the next summer.

Cortez loved seeing Winslow, and getting to know Daisy and Bloomfield. He had a wonderful visit. But after a while, Cortez began to miss his home in the shaggy old juniper tree. So he packed up his things, kissed Bloomfield and Daisy, and hugged Winslow goodbye.

Then Cortez the gnome headed home.

A NOTE ABOUT GNOMES:

When people think of gnomes, they tend to picture garden gnomes. Of course garden gnomes are just statues, and aren't like real gnomes at all. Real gnomes avoid people's houses and gardens, and never, ever wear red hats.

Gnomes are rare, but there are still a few out there.

If you ever meet a gnome, remember to treat them with the same respect you would show any grownup person. Never try to pick one up or put it in your pocket.